FIRST GRADE, HERE I COME!

NANCY CARLSON

PUFFIN BOOKS

To my first grade friends—
I hope you have fun in first grade, too!

PUFFIN BOOKS
Published by the Penguin Group
Penguin Young Readers Group, 345 Hudson Street, New York, New York 10014, U.S.A.
Penguin Group (Canada), 90 Eglinton Avenue East, Suite 700, Toronto, Ontario, Canada M4P 2Y3
(a division of Pearson Penguin Canada Inc.)
Penguin Books Ltd, 80 Strand, London WC2R 0RL, England
Penguin Ireland, 25 St Stephen's Green, Dublin 2, Ireland (a division of Penguin Books Ltd)
Penguin Group (Australia), 250 Camberwell Road, Camberwell, Victoria 3124, Australia
(a division of Pearson Australia Group Pty Ltd)
Penguin Books India Pvt Ltd, 11 Community Centre, Panchsheel Park, New Delhi – 110 017, India
Penguin Group (NZ), 67 Apollo Drive, Rosedale, North Shore 0632, New Zealand
(a division of Pearson New Zealand Ltd)
Penguin Books (South Africa) (Pty) Ltd, 24 Sturdee Avenue, Rosebank, Johannesburg 2196, South Africa

Registered Offices: Penguin Books Ltd, 80 Strand, London WC2R 0RL, England

First published in the United States of America by Viking, a division of Penguin Young Readers Group, 2006
Published by Puffin Books, a division of Penguin Young Readers Group, 2009

7 9 10 8

THE LIBRARY OF CONGRESS HAS CATALOGED THE VIKING EDITION AS FOLLOWS:
Carlson, Nancy L.
First grade, here I come! / written and illustrated by Nancy Carlson.
p. cm.
Summary: Henry tells his mother that he did not like his first day of first grade, but as he describes
what he did and learned, he begins to realize that he might enjoy it after all.
ISBN 0-670-06127-1 (hc)
[1. First day of school—Fiction. 2. Schools—Fiction.]
I. Title.
PZ7.C21665Fir 2006 [E]—dc22 2005023313

Puffin Books ISBN 978-0-14-241273-2

Manufactured in China
Set in Avenir
Book design by Kelley McIntyre

The first day of school was over, and when Henry got off the bus, his mother and little brother Pete were waiting for him. "How did you like first grade?" asked his mom.

"I didn't like it because I missed kindergarten," said Henry.
"Tell me all about it," said his mom.

"Well, my teacher isn't at all like my kindergarten teacher Ms. Bradley because . . .

"My first-grade teacher is a Mr.!

"But Mr. McCarthy likes my pet worm. And he even has a cool science corner with plants, bugs, rocks, and a guinea pig named Curly."

"The science corner sounds neat!" said Henry's mom.
"Where do you sit?"
"At my own desk that has my name on it."

"Do you sit near any of your friends?"
"No, I didn't know anyone in my class except Tony and Sydney from kindergarten. But guess what?

"I made a new friend named Oswaldo, and he sits next to me!

"Oswaldo likes soccer and spiders just like I do."

"He sounds nice. Did you learn anything new today?"
"Yes, we learned some math . . .

". . . some new songs with Ms. Cruse, and a science fact.

"Mr. McCarthy also took us to the library,

and he says soon we'll learn how to read books.
But today I already learned one word. . . .

"When I have to go to the bathroom, I look for the door that says B-O-Y-S.

"I also learned that when you open Curly's cage door . . .

" . . . he can run really fast!"

"Wow, you learned a lot! How was lunch?"

"The lunchroom was so big, and I was worried the food would be gross, but . . .

". . . tuna melts are really good."

"Did you go out for recess?"
"Yes, but the fifth graders hogged the monkey bars so . . ."

". . . Mr. McCarthy played kickball with us!"

"What did you do after recess?" asked his mom.

"We went to art class,

". . . we had a snack break,

and then I got sent to the principal's office," said Henry.
"Oh, no, did you get in trouble?"

"No, Mr. McCarthy asked me to deliver a note to the principal, and I didn't even get lost."

"Good for you!" said Henry's mom. "First grade does sound different from kindergarten."
"Yeah, but it's not too much for me, because . . .

"I'm a real first grader now!"

PR